TWO
BAD
ANTS

CHRIS VAN ALLSBURG

Houghton Mifflin Company

Boston

To Big C, the WFP

Library of Congress Cataloging-in-Publication Data

Van Allsburg, Chris.
   Two bad ants.

   Summary: When two bad ants desert from their
colony, they experience a dangerous adventure that
convinces them to return to their former safety.
   [1. Ants—Fiction] I. Title.
PZ7.V266Tw   1988   [E]   88-12988
ISBN 0-395-48668-8

Printed in the United States of America

HOR   10

TWO
BAD
ANTS

The news traveled swiftly through the tunnels of the ant world. A scout had returned with a remarkable discovery—a beautiful sparkling crystal. When the scout presented the crystal to the ant queen she took a small bite, then quickly ate the entire thing.

She deemed it the most delicious food she had ever tasted. Nothing could make her happier than to have more, much more. The ants understood. They were eager to gather more crystals because the queen was the mother of them all. Her happiness made the whole ant nest a happy place.

It was late in the day when they departed. Long shadows stretched over the entrance to the ant kingdom. One by one the insects climbed out, following the scout, who had made it clear—there were many crystals where the first had been found, but the journey was long and dangerous.

They marched into the woods that surrounded their underground home. Dusk turned to twilight, twilight to night. The path they followed twisted and turned, every bend leading them deeper into the dark forest.

More than once the line of ants stopped and anxiously listened for the sounds of hungry spiders. But all they heard was the call of crickets echoing through the woods like distant thunder.

Dew formed on the leaves above. Without warning, huge cold drops fell on the marching ants. A firefly passed overhead that, for an instant, lit up the woods with a blinding flash of blue-green light.

At the edge of the forest stood a mountain. The ants looked up and could not see its peak. It seemed to reach right to the heavens. But they did not stop. Up the side they climbed, higher and higher.

The wind whistled through the cracks of the mountain's face. The ants could feel its force bending their delicate antennae. Their legs grew weak as they struggled upward. At last they reached a ledge and crawled through a narrow tunnel.

When the ants came out of the tunnel they found themselves in a strange world. Smells they had known all their lives, smells of dirt and grass and rotting plants, had vanished. There was no more wind and, most puzzling of all, it seemed that the sky was gone.

They crossed smooth shiny surfaces, then followed the scout up a glassy, curved wall. They had reached their goal. From the top of the wall they looked below to a sea of crystals. One by one the ants climbed down into the sparkling treasure.

Quickly they each chose a crystal, then turned to start the journey home.
There was something about this unnatural place that made the ants nervous.
In fact they left in such a hurry that none of them noticed the two small ants
who stayed behind.

"Why go back?" one asked the other. "This place may not feel like home, but look at all these crystals." "You're right," said the other, "we can stay here and eat this tasty treasure every day, forever." So the two ants ate crystal after crystal until they were too full to move, and fell asleep.

Daylight came. The sleeping ants were unaware of changes taking place in their new found home. A giant silver scoop hovered above them, then plunged deep into the crystals. It shoveled up both ants and crystals and carried them high into the air.

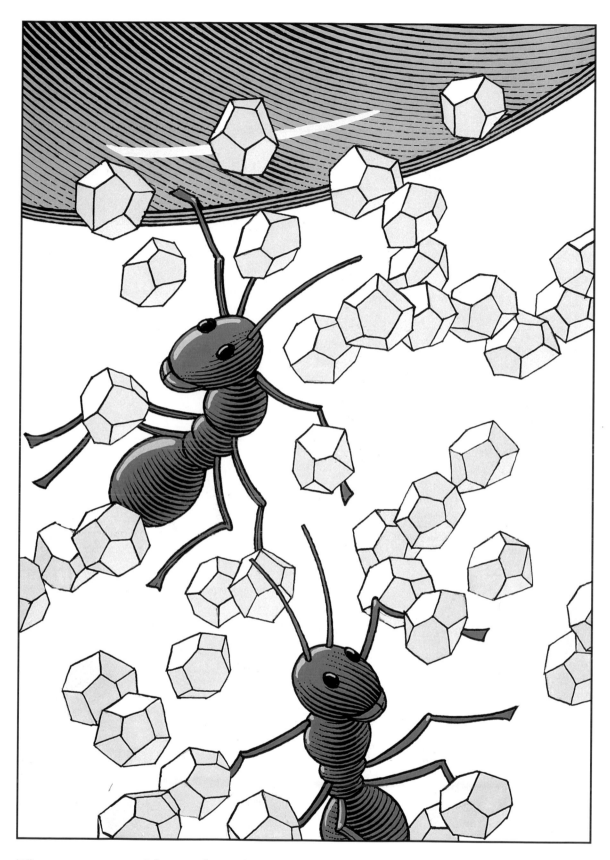

The ants were wide awake when the scoop turned, dropping them from a frightening height. They tumbled through space in a shower of crystals and fell into a boiling brown lake.

Then the giant scoop stirred violently back and forth. Crushing waves fell over the ants. They paddled hard to keep their tiny heads above water. But the scoop kept spinning the hot brown liquid.

Around and around it went, creating a whirlpool that sucked the ants deeper and deeper. They both held their breath and finally bobbed to the surface, gasping for air and spitting mouthfuls of the terrible, bitter water.

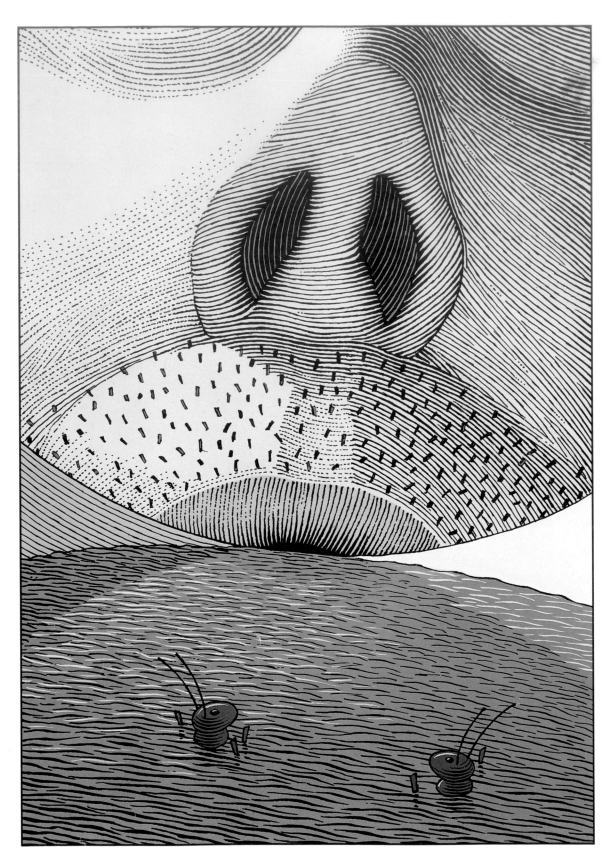

Then the lake tilted and began to empty into a cave. The ants could hear the rushing water and felt themselves pulled toward the pitch black hole. Suddenly the cave disappeared and the lake became calm. The ants swam to the shore and found that the lake had steep sides.

They hurried down the walls that held back the lake. The frightened insects looked for a place to hide, worried that the giant scoop might shovel them up again. Close by they found a huge round disk with holes that could neatly hide them.

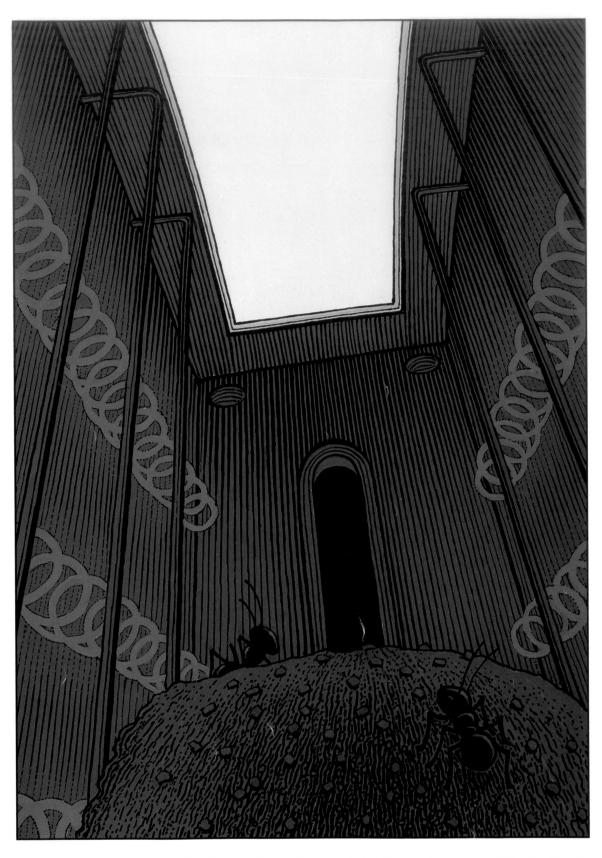

But as soon as they had climbed inside, their hiding place was lifted, tilted, and lowered into a dark space. When the ants climbed out of the holes they were surrounded by a strange red glow. It seemed to them that every second the temperature was rising.

It soon became so unbearably hot that they thought they would soon be cooked. But suddenly the disk they were standing on rocketed upward and the two hot ants went flying through the air.

They landed near what seemed to be a fountain—a waterfall pouring from a silver tube. Both ants had a powerful thirst and longed to dip their feverish heads into the refreshing water. They quickly climbed along the tube.

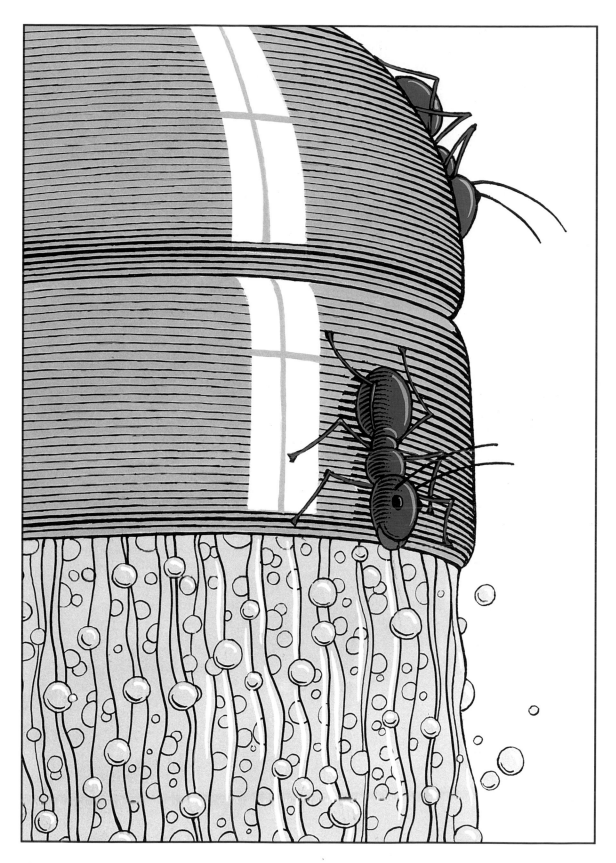

As they got closer to the rushing water the ants felt a cool spray. They tightly gripped the shiny surface of the fountain and slowly leaned their heads into the falling stream. But the force of the water was much too strong.

The tiny insects were pulled off the fountain and plunged down into a wet, dark chamber. They landed on half-eaten fruit and other soggy things. Suddenly the air was filled with loud, frightening sounds. The chamber began to spin.

The ants were caught in a whirling storm of shredded food and stinging rain. Then, just as quickly as it had started, the noise and spinning stopped. Bruised and dizzy, the ants climbed out of the chamber.

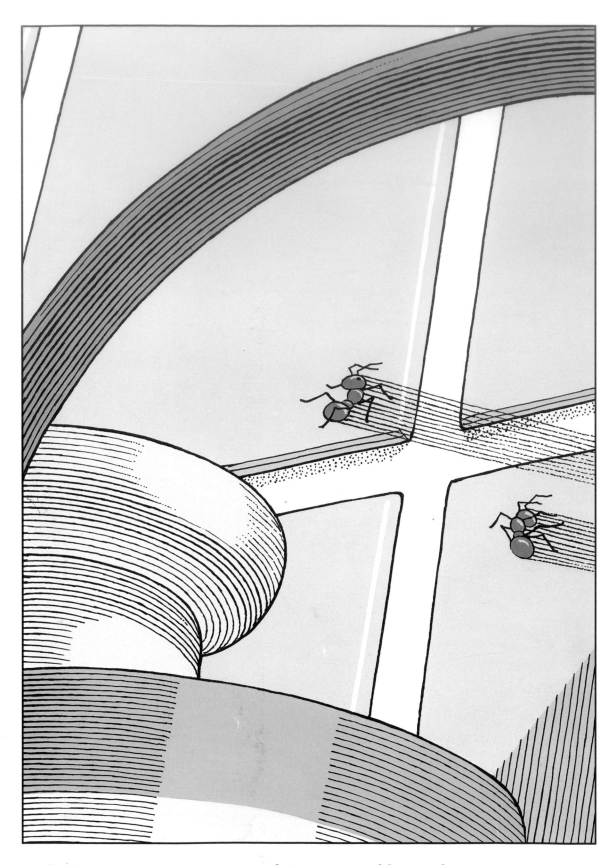

In daylight once again, they raced through puddles and up a smooth metal wall. In the distance they saw something comforting—two long, narrow holes that reminded them of the warmth and safety of their old underground home. They climbed up into the dark openings.

But there was no safety inside these holes. A strange force passed through the wet ants. They were stunned senseless and blown out of the holes like bullets from a gun. When they landed the tiny insects were too exhausted to go on. They crawled into a dark corner and fell fast asleep.

Night had returned when the battered ants awoke to a familiar sound—the footsteps of their fellow insects returning for more crystals. The two ants slipped quietly to the end of the line. They climbed the glassy wall and once again stood amid the treasure. But this time they each chose a single crystal and followed their friends home.

Standing at the edge of their ant hole, the two ants listened to the joyful sounds that came from below. They knew how grateful their mother queen would be when they gave her their crystals. At that moment, the two ants felt happier than they'd ever felt before. This was their home, this was their family. This was where they were meant to be.

The type is set in Garamond #3 by Composing Room of New England.
The paper is Futura Matte, supplied by Consolidated Papers.
Both text and jacket are printed by Acme Printing Company.
The books are bound by Horowitz/Rae.